To:

From:

*This coupon book is my gift to you—the biggest golf nut
I know. These coupons never expire and are
redeemable at any time by me.*

Golf

COUPONS

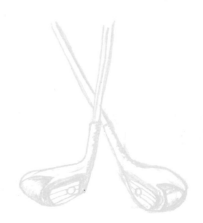

 Sourcebooks, Inc.
Naperville, IL

Published by Sourcebooks, Inc., P.O. Box 372, Naperville, IL 60566   (630) 961-3900   FAX: (630) 961-2168

Internal design and production by Andrew Sardina and Scott Theisen

Printed and bound in the United States of America.

10   9   8   7   6   5   4   3

Golf

This coupon is good for one free mulligan

C O U P O N S

Personal notes _____

_____

"If I'da cleared the trees and drove the green, it woulda been a great tee shot."

—Sam Snead

Golf

COUPONS

This coupon is good for one free two-putt

Personal notes

"Greens should be treated almost the same as water hazards: You land on them, then add two strokes to your score."

—Chi Chi Rodriguez

Golf

COUPONS

This coupon is good for one free one-putt

Personal notes

"Prayer never seems to work for me on the golf course. I think this has something to do with my being a terrible putter."

—Rev. Billy Graham

Golf

C O U P O N S

This coupon entitles
golfer to one free
foot wedge

Personal notes

"At first a golfer excuses a dismal performance by claiming bad lies. With experience, he covers up with better ones."

—P. Brown

Golf

COUPONS

This coupon entitles golfer to one free tee-up

Personal notes

"I'm hitting the woods just great, but I'm having a terrible time getting out of them."

—Harry Toscano

This coupon entitles golfer to one free "gimme" from anywhere on the green

Golf

C O U P O N S

Personal notes

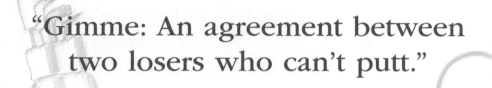

"Gimme: An agreement between two losers who can't putt."

—Jim Bishop

Golf

COUPONS

The Talented Golfer Coupon

Pretend I hit a draw (and kick my ball 10 yards to the left)

Personal notes

"Golf is the hardest game in the world to play and the easiest to cheat at."

—Dave Hill

Golf

C O U P O N S

The Talented Golfer Coupon

Pretend I hit a fade (and kick my ball 10 yards to the right)

Personal notes

"The only thing that you should force in a golf swing is the club back into the bag."

—Byron Nelson

Golf

COUPONS

This coupon entitles golfer to have "honors" on every hole today

Personal notes

"Good golfing temperament falls between taking it with a grin or shrug and throwing a fit."

—Sam Snead

Golf

C O U P O N S

This coupon entitles golfer to have "honors" on the hole of his or her choice

Personal notes _____

"What other people may find in poetry or art museums, I find in the flight of a good drive."

—Arnold Palmer

Golf

This coupon requires golf partner to search for lost golf balls (don't come back until you find three in good condition)

C O U P O N S

Personal notes

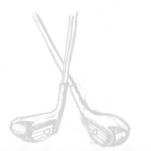

"It's good sportsmanship to not pick up lost golf balls while they are still rolling."

—Mark Twain

Best Ball Coupon

Mine are all skulled and
chipped, give me the
best ball in your bag

Golf

C O U P O N S

Personal notes

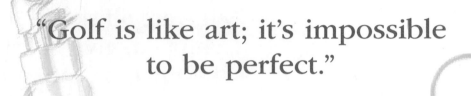

"Golf is like art; it's impossible to be perfect."

—Sandra Palmer

Golf

COUPONS

This coupon entitles golfer to take as many strokes in sand as necessary—but it counts as only one stroke

Personal notes _____

"It took me seventeen years to get three thousand hits in baseball. I did it in one afternoon on the golf course."

—Hank Aaron

Golf

COUPONS

This coupon entitles golfer to have an umbrella held over his/her head during rain or hot sun

Personal notes

"One thing that's always available on a golf course is advice."

—Buddy Hackett

Golf

COUPONS

This coupon entitles golfer to one bonus handicap stroke, taken in accordance with the course hole handicaps

Personal notes

"Never bet with anyone you meet on the first tee, who has a deep suntan, a one iron in his bag and squinty eyes."

—Dave Marr

This coupon entitles golfer
to one bonus handicap
stroke, taken on any hole
on the course

Golf

Personal notes

"You don't know what pressure is until you play for five bucks with only two in your pocket."

—Lee Trevino

Golf

COUPONS

This coupon requires golf partner to keep score (no cheating)

Personal notes

"The truly great things happen when a genius is alone. This is true especially among golfers."

—J.R. Coulson

Golf

This coupon entitles golfer to choose partner's club on his or her next shot

Personal notes

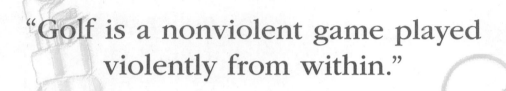

"Golf is a nonviolent game played violently from within."

—Bob Toski

Glf

This coupon entitles golfer
to play winter rules, while
partner plays regular rules

C O U P O N S

Personal notes

"Golf, in fact, is the only game in the world in which a precise knowledge of the rules can earn one a reputation for bad sportsmanship."

—Patrick Campbell

Golf

Get Out Of Sand Trap Free Coupon

C O U P O N S

Personal notes

"The game was easy for me as a kid, and I had to play a while to find out how hard it is."

—Raymond Floyd

Golf

This coupon
entitles golfer to play
the longest drive
of group

Personal notes

"Those who cannot drive suppose themselves to be good putters."

—Sir Walter Simpson

Golf

COUPONS

This coupon is good
for one free
practice putt

Personal notes

"The devoted golfer is an anguished soul who has learned a lot about putting just as an avalanche victim has learned a lot about snow."

—Dan Jenkins

Golf

This coupon entitles golfer
to choose who
drives the cart

Personal notes

"Real golfers go to work to relax."

—George Dillon

Golf

This coupon
entitles golfer to score
the whole round
without including putts

COUPONS

Personal notes _____

_____

"Golf is like fishing and hunting. What counts is the companionship and fellowship of friends, not what you catch or shoot."

—George Archer

Golf

C O U P O N S

This coupon is good for a free 250 yard drive

Personal notes

"You've just one problem. You stand too close to the ball—after you've hit it."

—Sam Snead

Golf

COUPONS

Get In Bounds Free
Coupon

Personal notes _____
_____

"No man has mastered golf until he has realized that his good shots are accidents and his bad shots good exercise."

—Eugene R. Black

Golf

COUPONS

This coupon entitles golfer to trade shots with another player

Personal notes

"To that man, age brought only golf instead of wisdom."

—George Bernard Shaw

The Concentration Coupon
This coupon entitles golfer to no talking during shot

Golf

C O U P O N S

Personal notes

"A golf course is the epitome of all that is purely transitory in the universe, a space not to dwell in, but to get over as quickly as possible."

—Jean Giraudoux

Golf

COUPONS

The No Concentration Coupon
I get to talk all the way
through your shot

Personal notes _____
_____

"He enjoys that perfect peace, that peace beyond all understanding, which comes at its maximum only to the man who has given up golf."

—P.G. Wodehouse

Golf

This coupon requires golf partner to rake coupon issuer's sand trap

Personal notes _____

_____

"A wife always knows when her husband has had a bad round. He has pond weed in his socks."

—P. Brown

Golf
COUPONS

This coupon entitles golfer
to use the red tees on the
hole of his or her choice

Personal notes

"I would rather play Hamlet with no rehearsal than play golf on television."

—Jack Lemmon

Golf

COUPONS

This coupon entitles golfer to use the red tees for the entire round today

Personal notes

"A hundred years of experience has demonstrated that the game is temporary insanity practiced in a pasture."

—Dave Kindred

Golf

Player of golfer's choice must use the blue tees

COUPONS

Personal notes

"The fun you get from golf is in direct ratio to the effort you don't put into it."

—Bob Allen

Golf

COUPONS

This coupon is good
for one free ball
throw from the tee

Personal notes

"It's a lot easier hitting a quarterback than a little white ball."

—Bubba Smith

Golf

COUPONS

This coupon is good for one free ball throw from a sand trap

Personal notes

"Always throw clubs ahead of you. That way you don't have to waste energy going back to pick them up."

—Tommy Bolt

Golf

C O U P O N S

Recipient of coupon must tee off with 9 iron

Personal notes _____

_____

"I play with friends, but we don't play friendly games."

—Ben Hogan

Golf

COUPONS

Recipient of coupon
must tee off with
7 iron

Personal notes

"Golf is a game whose aim is to hit a very small ball into an even smaller hole, with weapons singularly ill-designed for the purpose."

—Sir Winston Churchill

Golf

C O U P O N S

Recipient of coupon must tee off with 5 iron

Personal notes

"Golf is so popular simply because it is the best game in the world at which to be bad."

—A.A. Milne

Golf

C O U P O N S

Recipient of coupon
must tee off with
2 iron

Personal notes _____

"I know I'm getting better at golf because I'm hitting fewer spectators."

—Gerald R. Ford

Golf

The No Practice Swings Coupon
Just hit the ball!

Personal notes _____
_____

"If you watch a game, it's fun. If you play it, it's recreation. If you work at it, it's golf."

—Bob Hope

Golf

The Pencil Iron Coupon.
Golfer may drop his or
her score from a double
bogie to a bogie

Personal notes

"Golf is a game in which you yell Fore, shoot six, and write down five."

—Paul Harvey

Golf

C O U P O N S

The Pencil Iron Coupon

Golfer may drop his or her score from a bogie to a par

Personal notes _____

"Good golf isn't a matter of hitting great shots. It's finding a way to make your bad ones not so bad."

—Lee Trevino

Golf

COUPONS

The Pencil Iron Coupon
Golfer may drop his or her
score from a par to a birdie

Personal notes

"Golf combines two favorite American pastimes: taking long walks and hitting things with a stick."

—P.J. O'Rourke

Golf

COUPONS

Player of golfer's choice must use a range ball off the next tee

Personal notes

"Everyone gets wounded in a game of golf. The trick is not to bleed."

—Peter Dobereiner

Golf

C O U P O N S

Player of golfer's choice must use a range ball on the next green

Personal notes _____
_____

"The biggest liar in the world is the golfer who claims that he plays the game merely for exercise."

—Tommy Bolt

This coupon disallows
golf partner from
using a tee on their
next drive

Golf
C O U P O N S

Personal notes

"All truly great golf courses have an almost supernatural finishing hole, by way of separating the chokers from the strokers."

—Charles Price

Golf

This coupon entitles golfer
to all coins used by others
as ball markers during
today's round

C O U P O N S

Personal notes

"The person I fear most in the last two rounds is myself."

—Tom Watson

The No Snowmen Coupon.
This coupon entitles
golfer to score all
eights as sevens during
today's round

Personal notes

"You don't necessarily have to bring your clubs to play golf—just lie about your score."

—Lon Simmons

Golf

The I'm Away Coupon.
This coupon requires golfer's
partner to putt first, even if he or
she is away

Personal notes

"I'd give up golf if I didn't have so many sweaters."

—Bob Hope

Golf

C O U P O N S

This coupon entitles
golfer to recrop
without penalty

Personal notes

"The difference between a sand trap and water is the difference between a car crash and an airplane crash. You have a chance of recovering from a car crash."

—Bobby Jones

Golf

This coupon entitles golfer to throw out the hole

COUPONS

Personal notes _____

_____

"Golf is a game of expletives not deleted."

—Dr. Irving A. Gladstone

This coupon requires
partner to play
without spikes in his
or her golf shoes

Golf

C O U P O N S

Personal notes

"Golf got complicated when I had to wear shoes and begin thinking about what I was doing."

—Sam Snead

Golf

COUPONS

This coupon requires game loser to buy a subscription to a golf magazine for the winner

Personal notes

"That little white ball won't move until you hit it, and there's nothing you can do after it has gone."

—Babe Didrikson Zaharias

Golf

The I'm Sick Today Coupon.
Call my office, I'm
going golfing instead

COUPONS

Personal notes

"My worst day on the golf course still beats my best day in the office."

—John Hallisey

Golf

Bonus Mulligan.
This coupon is good
for one free mulligan

COUPONS

Personal notes _____

_____

"Mulligan: Invented by an Irishman who wanted to hit one more twenty-yard grounder."

—Jim Bishop

Golf

COUPONS

Bonus Two-Putt.
This coupon is
good for one free
two-putt

Personal notes _____

"Even when times were good, I realized that my earning power as a golf professional depended on too many ifs and putts."

—Gene Sarazen

Bonus One-Putt.
This coupon is good for one free one-putt

Golf

COUPONS

Personal notes

"The trouble with golf is you're only as good as your last putt."

—Doug Sanders

Bonus Foot Wedge.
This coupon entitles
golfer to one free
foot wedge

Golf

C O U P O N S

Personal notes

"You know the old rule. He who have fastest cart never have to play bad lie."

—Mickey Mantle

Golf

COUPONS

Bonus Tee-Up.

This coupon entitles golfer

to one free tee-up

Personal notes

"I don't say my golf game is bad; but if I grew tomatoes, they'd come up sliced."

—Miller Barber

Bonus Gimme.
This coupon entitles
golfer to one free
"gimme" from anywhere
on the green

Personal notes

"A good player who is a great putter is a match for any golfer. A great hitter who cannot putt is a match for no one."

—Ben Sayers

Send us your coupon idea!

What do you most want to give to your favorite golfer? Golfers, what do you really want from your loved ones? Send us your coupon ideas—if we use them in our next book or in future editions, we'll send you a free copy of the finished book! Submission of ideas implies free and clear permission to use in any and all future editions. Send your coupons to:

Sourcebooks
Attn: Coupon Ideas
P.O. Box 372
Naperville, IL 60566

My Ideas